St. Lawrence Seaway

Quebec City

Montreal

Thousand Islands

Charlottetown

Halifax

North
Atlantic Ocean

North

West · East

South

The name "Tallulah" is of Native American origin and means "leaping water."

For Theresa, a gem of a sister.
And John, for believing in mermaids.
Denise Brennan-Nelson

For Candy and in loving memory of Bob.
In honor of my mermaid Ava.
SKH

Sleeping Bear Press®
2395 South Huron Parkway, Suite 200
Ann Arbor, MI 48104
www.sleepingbearpress.com

Printed and bound in the United States.

10 9 8 7 6 5 4 3 2 1

Library of Congress Cataloging-in-Publication Data
Brennan-Nelson, Denise.
Tallulah : mermaid of the Great Lakes / by Denise Brennan-Nelson ;
illustrated by Susan Kathleen Hartung.
pages cm
Summary: "Tallulah the mermaid realizes that she is different from the other
mermaids in the ocean and finds that she truly belongs in the Great Lakes"
— Provided by publisher.
ISBN 978-1-58536-909-6
[1. Mermaids—Fiction. 2. Individuality—Fiction. 3. Great Lakes (North America)—Fiction.]
I. Hartung, Susan Kathleen, illustrator. II. Title.
PZ7.B75165Tal 2015
[E]—dc23   2014027165

Tallulah

Mermaid of the Great Lakes

By Denise Brennan-Nelson • Illustrated by Susan Kathleen Hartung

According to ancient mythology, every mermaid has a special gemstone hidden somewhere in the sea. Once a mermaid finds it, her tail will take on the same color as the stone and she will acquire her magical powers. Her powers are used to help fisherman and freighters during storms, safeguard treasures in sunken ships, maintain lighthouses, and awaken imaginations with enchanting melodies.

In the blue, shallow water of the sea a group of young mermaids splashed in the waves. Their tails shimmered in the summer sun, hinting at the jeweled colors they would soon become.

But when Tallulah waved her dull, gray tail back and forth to catch the sunlight, it didn't sparkle and the other mermaids giggled. Tallulah quickly hid her tail in the water.

Finally, the day had arrived! Sea creatures from all over gathered to wish the young mermaids luck in their search.

Tallulah listened and watched as the elder mermaid gave instructions and advice to the young mermaids about where and how to search for their gemstones.

When Tallulah tried to ask a question, they all stared at her dull, gray tail and said nothing.

After just a few weeks of searching, the young mermaids returned, excited to show off their colorful gems and sparkling tails.

But weeks and months floated by with no sign of Tallulah.

It had been almost a year when Tallulah returned.
Her tail was the same dull color it had always been.
The sea creatures gathered around her.

Exhausted and sad, Tallulah whispered:

"I've searched in every ocean.
I've been to every sea.
I cannot find my gem;
wherever can it be?"

The elder mermaid spoke
in a raspy, stern voice:

*"No ocean holds your gem,
nor any sea of blue.
Search no more, Tallulah;
there is no gem for you!"*

The words fell like an
anchor around Tallulah.

Sea Turtle's deep voice interrupted the silence.
"Have you looked in the Great Lakes?"

"The *what*?" Seahorse exclaimed.

"Never heard of 'em," Octopus grumbled.

"That's ridiculous!" The elder mermaid scolded Turtle.
"Lakes don't need mermaids. Mermaids live in the ocean!"

"Yeah," a young mermaid said, rolling her eyes. "And
lakes don't have gemstones."

"These lakes are special and more beautiful than you
could ever imagine," Turtle said.

Tallulah listened intently as Sea Turtle
told her about the Great Lakes.

"Will you take me there?" Tallulah asked.

Turtle nodded, "But I can't
stay for long."

In the wee hours of the morning, Turtle and Tallulah set off for the Great Lakes.

Side by side they swam until they felt a change in the water.

"The Great Lakes are not far from here," Turtle told her.

"Do you really think I'll find my gemstone?" Tallulah asked.

Glancing at her dull, gray tail, Turtle nodded.

Tallulah was anxious to begin searching for her gem. They swam through locks, and past ports and islands until they reached Lake Ontario.

They spent the day searching islands and shipwrecks as a school of curious bluegill followed closely behind.

They swam by big cities,

lighthouses,

and sandy bluffs.

Peeking over the edge of a rock they watched bicycles
and horse-drawn carriages circle around an island.

For days, Tallulah looked everywhere for her gemstone!

"Brrrrr… it's chilly," Tallulah shivered as they swam into Lake Superior. But she loved the feel of the cool, blue water.

She explored cliffs and arches. She dove deep in the water hoping to find her gemstone at the bottom of a waterfall, but it wasn't there.

Tallulah and Turtle swam for miles and miles, searching for her gemstone.

Tired and heartbroken, Tallulah found a cove to rest in.

Watching the moon rise above the water, her hopes of finding her gemstone sank.

Tallulah turned to Turtle: "These lakes are even more beautiful than you described. I wish I could stay here forever. But I should have listened to the other mermaids. There is no gem for me. Maybe it's time we went home," she said with a wistful sigh.

"There is one more lake," Turtle said, glancing at her tail.

Early the next day, Tallulah and Turtle set off
to explore Lake Michigan.

They searched for her gemstone around islands and sand
dunes … past big-city shorelines and quaint ones, too.

Soon, they were playing in marinas and harbors... around piers, under docks, and rafts... they counted lighthouses... chased ferry boats and yachts ... hung out in the bay... they played tag with schools of fish...

...swam near white sandy beaches sprinkled with beach chairs and umbrellas...floated on their backs and watched kites diving and twirling in the sky and sun-kissed children building sculptures out of sand.

At the end of the day, Tallulah and Turtle drifted in the gentle waves and watched the sun sparkle across the water.

Tallulah had been having so much fun that she hadn't thought about finding her gemstone all day.

"Thank you, Turtle," she said. "I forgot how much fun it is to be a mermaid."

The sound of children playing on the beach reached Tallulah and she was curious to get a better look at their sand castles.

They waited until the beaches were empty before making their way to shore.

They were admiring the sand castles the children had built when something caught Tallulah's eye. It looked oddly familiar.

Tallulah reached out to pick it up.

As soon as she saw the beautiful sunburst pattern of the Petoskey stone, Tallulah realized what it was.

Holding it out for Turtle to see, Tallulah exclaimed, "I found it, Turtle! I found my gemstone!"

"Yes, you did, Tallulah," Turtle replied. "And the Great Lakes found their mermaid."

The next time you are near one of the Great Lakes,
listen carefully and you might hear Tallulah singing….

There are mermaids in the ocean
And mermaids in the sea.
But here among the Great Lakes
Is where I'm meant to be.

"*Everything you can imagine is real.*"
—Pablo Picasso

Duluth

Isle Royale

Lake Superior

Marquette

Pictured Rocks

Sault Ste. Marie

Mackinac Island

Alpena

Lake Huron

Green Bay

Sleeping Bear Dunes

Traverse City

Tawas

Bay City

Toronto

Lake Ontario

Muskegon

Milwaukee

Lake Michigan

Niagara Fall.

Buffalo

Holland

Sarnia

Detroit

Lake Erie

Chicago

Gary

Toledo

Cleveland